HUNTER
Who #1

HUNTER
Who #1

by Louis W. J. Uthoff

ASA PUBLISHING CORPORATION
AN INNOVATIVE OUTSOURCE BOOK PUBLISHING HYBRID

ASA Publishing Corporation
1285 N. Telegraph Rd., #376, Monroe, Michigan 48162
An Accredited Publishing House with the BBB
www.asapublishingcorporation.com

Copyrights©2021, Louis W. J. Uthoff, All Rights Reserved
Book Title: Hunter Who #1
Date Published: 09.14.2021 / Edition 1 *Trade Paperback*
Book ID: ASAPCID2380815
ISBN: 978-1-946746-87-0
Library of Congress Cataloging-in-Publication Data

This book was published in the United States of America.
Great State of Michigan

Table of Contents

PREFACE

Hunter Who #1

A long time ago in a dimension far far away. The Queen Republic lost her first world war, she went into a new dimension where a planet called Earth has been taken captive under her siege. The Queen Republic sent her army to attack the villages. But not long ago, the villages got overran and had been infected by the Queen Republic's army.

One of the battle cruiser's crew found a little baby, but he appeared to be a human baby boy, and his skin was like dragon skin. So they took the boy to the queen. Examining this half-breed, the queen decided to take interest in him. The queen then ordered the battle cruiser crew to be executed and quickly took the baby to train him.

The pupp grew up and was trained in hand-to-hand combat by the queen's most top warriors. The young boy (pupp) was only allowed to be trained, using only human weapons. After the young boy's training was done the queen gave the boy a suit and armor to attack other dimensions, and he succeeded. The queen now has a full army and super weapons. She declared a second war, so she sent out with the first wave of her army across the Atlantic Ocean to attack America. Then the rest of the army began attacking the rest of the world. The queen now becoming triumphant in her quest, centered her backup army and her super weapons to Columbus, Ohio to get the upper hand.

This is the story of *Hunter Who #1* . . .

HUNTER
Who #1

CHAPTER 1
Battlefield

The sky was full of dark clouds and a ship was flying in a downward spiral. Bullets were flying from the inside of another gunship. It was a group of ten pupps and the Captain of the descending ship, along with two pilots.

The Captain shouted to them, "Okay team, we have humans on the ground, I want you to make a spot for our ship to land," he turns to look at the pilots, "and to send it back up." The Captain then shouted, "WE GOT IT!?"

The pupps and the two pilots yelled in a strong response, "YES, SIR!"

The ship began flying lower and lower, and then it had finally touched the ground. When the doors began to open up, the pupps started running out with guns blazing; bullets were flying everywhere. The pupps immediately had to run to the first trench. They knew that staying down was the best defense for now because there was a continual array of bullets passing over them.

An hour later, the gunfire had stopped, and then the pupps moved very fast to the next trench. Hunter was a little farther ahead, leading the battalion of pupps. He knew they had to move quickly on the ground because it would not take long for the humans to reload their weapons. Then all of a sudden, Hunter heard another round of gunfire. As soon as he looked to see, an explosion of rocks and gravel. The rocks were splattering up and off the ground. The bullets ripping right beside him. Hunter couldn't stay in that same spot any longer. So he immediately got up and kept running, but he ran faster than usual because he knew that if he stopped, the humans could pull back when the tank burst open, and there would be a big black dragon with muscles walking on all four legs coming out. Unfortunately, it was too late; the black dragon had already burst out and broke the line. All of the pupps were left with no choice and had to run to the last trench hole where the other humans were. Hunter seeing the digger working, wanted to hold on and get the Queen's Soldiers through. Hunter and the other pupps had looked back at the Queen's Soldiers. The soldiers were running straight ahead, then looked towards the frontline and saw the humans running away.

Fifteen hours and twenty-eight minutes later, Hunter and the other pupps went back into the hole. They were waiting for the drop-off ship.

One pupp asked Hunter, "What does the Queen's castle look like?"

Hunter happily said, "It's looking good, it's white and blue." The pupp's eyes grew bigger in amazement, and while Hunter continued talking, a loud voice came out from one of the soldiers. The soldier peeked his head inside the trench hole and yelled, "Okay pupps, we need to do another breach." The soldier then walks over to Hunter, "I need your pupps to get ready." Hunter and the pupps agreed and walked out of the hole and made a line for another run attack. When the other pupps showed up, Hunter looked at them and pulled out his pistol. The pupps did the same as the other pupps did as they got closer.

This is the line that was drawn between humans and infections. Then one of the infections screamed, and then the Queen's Republic Soldiers charged, and the pupps did the same. Hunter started running as fast as he could until he made it to the front of the line. Hunter jumped and landed on a human soldier's face. Hunter pulled his gun out and started firing. Hunter shot and killed the soldier. As the battle was raging on, human soldiers were trying to help one another against Hunter, but he was too fast. He clawed and scratched other soldiers with one paw, and shooting with the other killing them in droves. Hunter used a knife from a dead soldier and threw it at another soldier's head, killing him. The line was now overran by the Queen's Republic Soldiers.

Six minutes later, Hunter sits on the

ground leaning his back up against a wall waiting for the next sound attack; when one of the Queen's Republic Soldiers walks up to Hunter and looks down at him.

Queen Republic Soldier said, "Hunter, . . ."

Hunter looked at the soldier and asked, "What is it?"

"The Queen needs to talk to you about twenty more invasions and, that you did a good job in your mission," continued the soldier.

Hunter looks at the empty line. "Are you guys going to be okay with pushing up for some more?"

One of the Queen's Soldiers said, "Yes! We'll be fine! The other army is still pushing forward, and this time we're going to win the front like the last war - but this time with more force on those humans!"

Hunter gets up and hears the drop-off ship land. Hunter walked to the frontline wall and moved up to climb over it. Hunter then walked to the drop-off ship and got in. The drop-off ship took off flying up pass clouds, all way to the atmosphere, and then within the clouds appeared another drop where they can land on a landing pad.

CHAPTER 2

Hunter Meets Ship

The Drop off ship opens the door, and Hunter walks out and sees a big wall in front of him. It's a very huge wall with the same two doors. Hunter steps up to the doors but not too close. He then hears the Queen's guard talking.

The Queen's guard said, "Mogot se mouk."

Then Hunter replied, "Ji po Hunter."

In response, the Queen's guard said, "Welcome home, Hunter," then the two doors began to open. Once they were opened, Hunter could see the city and its buildings. They were in the areas where the families; mothers and pupps were resting while every father goes out to fight the second war, and then there are other buildings that store food because the Queen knows how it is dangerous for the families to go out and try to find food during the time of battle. So, the Queen's Soldiers went out and found the food for them, taking it away from the humans and bringing the food into the Queen's Republic. The water on the Queen's Republic is not infected. The fish are able to reproduce. However, the soldiers are bringing in cows, pigs, chickens, and other food to feed their pupps.

While walking out into the city, Hunter goes pass the Queen's citizens to the castle where she resides, as he approaches the two front doors, they began to open the doors. As the doors were opening all the way and they came to a full stop, Hunter was greeted by a dragon-man standing in the middle of the citizens.

"You did well in your second mission," Jeilrenth said. Then he continued, "The Queen wants to talk to you about the next mission."

Hunter and Jeilrenth walked in together, and the doors began closing right behind them. They continued down the hallway corridor until they reached the throne. When they arrived, the Queen was sitting on her throne looking at Hunter as he walked in. Jeilrenth looked over at Hunter, then Jeilrenth turned back to face the Queen and voiced out his introduction to the Queen.

"My Queen, his second mission was successful. The humans pulled back."

"A good team! He gets his gift," the Queen bellowed.

Hunter looked at the Queen and bowed as she was getting up, and then stood back up as she began walking towards them, standing in front of her throne at a distance from them, in the middle of the room.

After approaching Hunter and Jeilrenth, the Queen stared back at Hunter and said, "Hunter, come." Then she looked over at her door guard, "Jeilrenth, go back to your station until someone sends for you."

"Yes, my Queen," responded Jeilrenth."

Then Jeilrenth bowed for a few seconds, stood back up, turned around and began walking towards the doors. Hunter and the Queen turned toward the walkway of the throne and began walking down the hallway together.

While walking, the Queen began talking to Hunter. "I saw everything that you did, and your training is paying off."

"Yes, it is my Queen."

Still walking, Hunter began gazing around, they both continued talking.

The Queen slowed her walking down a little more and says, "I still have this gift for you."

Hunter asks, "What is it?"

Hunter and the Queen step out of the hallway and then made it into the Queen's garden. The Queen and Hunter stopped walking for a few moments while looking at the lovely garden.

"Hunter, you are my true soldier," complimented the Queen.

"Yes, my queen, I will be yours forever," responded Hunter.

The Queen was blushing then she sexually smacks his butt. Hunter looking peculiar, doesn't know why she did that. After a little screech of giggle coming out through the Queen's hands over her mouth, she stops blushing, then she and Hunter walk out of the garden together.

As they continue walking back out in the hallway and down the corridor, they see *the Collectors* surrounding this big machine-looking type of box, resembling one of their spaceships. This machine is just standing there doing nothing as Hunter and the Queen tour around this monstrosity.

"Is that one of the Collectors?" asked Hunter. "Because it sure looks like they have one of our spaceships." He then breaks away from the Queen for a few minutes to examine this machine. While Hunter was looking at it, he becomes more curious, seeing that the outside of it appears to be all metal.

Hunter looks at one of them. "Hey, Collector! It looks like a ship; how can I get into one of these and take a look around inside?"

The Collectors look at each other then tried to think about how to open this metal box, that they are surrounding, which appears to look like it is a ship of some type.

Hunter asks another question, "Where did this ship come from?"

All the Collectors said in unison, "We don't know where it came from. We found it floating in space, and we towed it here."

Just then, the metal walls fell apart in

sections, and the ship's doors open up like a garage door going up. Hunter in amazement walks up to the ship and peeks inside with just a glimpse. Hunter noticed that there was a computer plug on a table. The computer plug had a lot of control buttons and a leaver. Hunter then fully walks inside and sees that the roof has two large holes. Then Hunter ask himself, "What are these holes being left open like this? . . . Hmmm . . ."

Then, all of a sudden, the ship itself begins to speak. "These holes are left for the gunners."

Everyone froze because now this ship is not only showing that it's active, but that it can talk. Hunter breaks everyone's silence by responding to the ship. "Hello, . . . who are you?"

The box-type-looking ship responded, "Well, I have no name, but you can name me, Sir."

Hunter looks at the Queen and the Collectors in awe. Then, as he begins to slightly turn his head back around, in the middle of the table a robot's head is rising and turning to look right back at Hunter. Hunter then staring back - looks at it and says, "Can I call you, *Ship*?"

The robot-head took a while to respond but then said, "Yes," in acceptance.

Hunter then looked at two holes near and above him, smiles, and said with excitement, "Sweet! Two gunners, this is going to be fun for humans!"

The two ladders drop down, and then Hunter grabs one of them and climbs the ladder to the top of the ship. *Ship* is now obeying Hunter's commands. The Queen and the Collectors are still outside of the box-looking type ship trying to figure out what just happened.

Collector One said, "That ship talks, and it sounds like factious."

Collector Two in somewhat agreement, "That factious has weapons on it."

The Queen responded in concern, "That ship has not kill us yet."

The next thing you know, the guns were discharging, and shooting in the air from the roof, then they stopped. Next, you can see Hunter sliding down on this retractable ladder, yelling, "Ah man, that was fun!"

The Queen makes a facial expression towards the Collectors as they have now ended their conversation and is directing her attention back towards Hunter.

"I see that you have given it a new name, so what do you think about Ship?"

Hunter, still with his adrenaline on high, responded, "She'll do, and this ship would help me with two gunners."

"Then Ship, burst into an interruption of their conversation and said, "I have more than just two gunners." As Ship was saying this, the back of the ship begins opening. Hunter looking in shock, then blurted out,

"You are full of more surprises!"

Then one of the Queen's Soldiers came in and ran directly to her. "My Queen, there are a lot of humans on the ground forming one major line!"

The Queen said out loud with anger, "How did that happen?! Their two sides came together to win the war!"

The soldier and Collectors look at each other with fear, but then Hunter speaks out, "I will help the first wave."

Then the Queen turned around to look at Hunter. A few minutes went by, and then her anger begins to fade away. A decision has been made. "Fine, you must help our soldiers push our enemies back."

Hunter responded, "Yes, my Queen."

"One more thing," the Queen presses decisively, "Hunter, start getting my soldiers ready!"

CHAPTER 3

Hunter Arm

Hunter and the other Queen's Soldiers were getting ready for reinforcements to help the first wave.

Hunter yells, "COME ON - COME ON!"

The soldiers at once get into the ship at Hunter's command. Hunter then looks around to see if anyone else is coming. One pupp shows up, the same with the other ten pupps following. The ship closes its doors, then takes off. Hunter and everyone else was very quiet, but then Hunter begins to speak.

"Okay soldiers, this is the first wave. Somehow, our soldiers got ambushed by the humans, so our mission is to help out our fellow soldiers, to fight back for the Queen Republic, now who's with me?!" The Queen's Soldiers' dragon roared.

The ship started flying downward then suddenly bullets were hitting the ship, but there was no visible marks and no physical damages. The ship landed and then opened its doors. The Queen's Soldiers were running out of the ship attacking the humans. The last soldier running out of the ship was

Hunter. There was exploding gunfire surrounding the humans causing the death of humans. The humans began to surrender to the Queen's Soldiers. The sky is being blackened by smoke. Hunter ran up and punched a human soldier in the face and ripped out his larynx, then he went to seize his gun. The gun is a Class M4 with a Grenade Launcher. Hunter grabs it and starts to open fire, killing forty human soldiers. Then he heard a voice out of nowhere, it sounded like, "Hunter, Stop!" Hunter looked around and seen the Queen's Soldiers' killing human soldiers. Hunter then heard the sound of a baby crying.

Hunter was having flashbacks, remembering about his first mission; a

Queen's soldier walking by with a stroller and hearing a baby crying in it. So as he turned around gazing into this glimpsed portion of his past, it was also making him remember and causing him to freeze as he's visualizing a Queen's soldier who scratched the baby and killed it. Then seeing this, the Queen's soldier grab the baby and started walking back to the Queen Republic ship and getting on it, then heading back to the Queen Republic to raise it. Hunter snapped out of it and went back to killing the human soldiers.

Five hours later, the humans were losing ground, Hunter and his Queen's Soldiers are at the frontline helping soldiers from the first wave. Hunter was on the line shooting at the human soldiers killing them all, then another voice came out of nowhere.

"Leave! You need to leave before it's too late!"

Then another voice came from nowhere as well and said, "Shut up you scum!"

Then . . . BOOM!!!

The explosion almost destroyed the entire area, killing almost everyone and everything in its path. Hunter looked around and saw the bodies of some of the Queen's Soldiers and human soldiers together laying there dead. Hunter knows that something is happening, then he hears another voice but he doesn't understand it, then a real voice bellowed out.

"Sir, we gotta pull back!"

Hunter looked toward the left side of him and saw that that one pupp earlier yelled, "We need to pull back!"

Hunter then yelling in response, "Ok! Let's pull back!"

The humans and pupps were running toward the ship, but the car was not so far from them and exploded as well. The debris was flying everywhere; a large chunk of it flying through the air towards one of the pupps. Hunter had a feeling that he should go save him. So, running towards him, not thinking, Hunter pushes the pupp out of the way, then debris hit Hunter instead - cutting his skin all way through. Hunter lost his right arm and dropped to the ground screaming in pain. The one pupp that Hunter saved looked at the ship which was at a little distance off, the pupp turned back around and stared at Hunter as Hunter was crying in agony. The pupp ran towards him and grabs Hunter by the waistline and his other arm. The pupp lifts Hunter up and tries to make an attempt to get him back to the ship. The pupp made it all way to the ship with Hunter continually screaming in pain, but Hunter could still hear the pupp who saved him.

"We need to take you back to the Queen right way!"

As Hunter was slowly drifting into unconsciousness; his eyes beginning to get a little heavy, he sees this big woman with golden hair wearing a golden chiton and a long golden cape staring back at him with fear before finally blacking out.

CHAPTER 4

Duel of Hunter

Hunter, while still passed out, the engineers took him from where he was laying at. The engineers placed him on the table to examine his right shoulder because of the massive damage that he sustained from the debris, which caused the loss of his arm.

While one engineer was observing, he said, "How is this possible? Look, here's a viral infection that he got, it made the upper part of his right arm grow back, but for some reason it didn't affect the other arm."

The other Engineer standing beside him responded, "Well, what do you know, it only grew to a nice size stubble; a healthy one at that. I'll alert the queen and see if she would allow us to repair this arm."

A few minutes later, the engineer came back informing the other engineers to go ahead with the cyborg arm transplant, but the queen also ordered them to weaponize it; make his new arm a weapon.

They all nodded in agreement and began getting their surgery equipment and a cyborg arm that was inside of this long metallic casing.

A second engineer squeezed the stub to see if the virus infection completely stopped and that there were no other abnormalities.

"We're good here, let's go ahead and recut the dried virus patches near the shoulder blades so we can clamp it on without any complications."

The third Engineer holding Hunter's new cyborg arm replied, "We have to rally together so we can do a test on this arm."

Four engineers, once again, all agreed together after the last engineer said that they would go ahead and test it.

When the initial Engineer pressed the test button the cyborg arm began to vibrate a little, then it started sparking. Everything stopped, briefly for a moment, where the only thing you could see are small streams of smoke. All of a sudden as the Engineer holding the arm begins to look away, sparks started getting more intensely worst; popping and crackling, it was like a lightshow; sparks flying everywhere. The engineer who was holding the new arm reached over and had to turn it off quickly before it becomes permanently damaged beyond repair, and then proceeded back to the workshop to look at exactly what went wrong.

Hunter still passed out for a while from surgery. Just then, two light balls came out of his body; one dark red, and the other is light. Then, the two balls *turned into spirts*, they both looked like Hunter.

The Dark Spirit yelled at the Light Spirit, "YOU HAVE TO GET AWAY, TELL HIM TO RUN!"

The Light spirit is being scared about what the Dark spirit said, wondering what he's going to do with him.

The Dark spirit kept yelling, "IF YOU HAVE NOT SAVED THAT DAMN PUPP, THEN HIS ARM WOULD NOT BE CUT OFF!"

The Dark spirit then looked at Hunter as the Light spirit became even more scared, but he had a feeling that he had never felt before. When he heard a voice while looking down, he saw a light sword, then another voice said to Light, "You did the right thing to save that pupp, now it's time you save

Hunter's life."

Light said in his head about how Dark is so powerful, that he can't stand it. Then a voice interrupted and said, "Light, you are Hunter, you are Hunter's spirit. You bring hope to him and to stop the Dark Hunter before he corrupts Hunter."

Dark Hunter being used to his dark power going inside Hunter, but now he felt a stronger air pressure pushing him away from Hunter, who is currently lying unconscious unaware of what's going on over him. Dark Hunter unbalanced by the air's compression hit the wall and fell to the ground.

Dark Hunter looking up at Light Hunter saw something he never saw before - Light Hunter is brave!

Dark Hunter yelled, "What are you doing you stupid little . . .!"

Light Hunter interrupted by saying, "Shush, you murderer!"

The Dark Hunter looked in shock staring at Light Hunter realizes that the Light Hunter had power, but how? He never had learned about them, so where did the power come from? The Dark Hunter knows now that the fight over Hunter is just beginning. The Dark Hunter gets up and pulls out his black and bloody sword, then the Light Hunter pulls his clean sword out. The Light Hunter's sword is golden, and the middle is blue.

The Dark Hunter in rage charges at the Light Hunter, but the Light Hunter moves to the left causing Dark Hunter to miss and hit a saw machine, destroying it. The Dark and Light Hunter's sword swing, clanging and crashing each other from right to left, up and down, side to side, and across the Light Hunter straight upward and the Dark Hunter on the other side holding it. Just then another sword flew pass Dark Hunter's face. Both, Dark Hunter and Light Hunter stopped and look at where this sword was coming from. All of a sudden they saw it - another Spirit of Hunter standing.

Dark Hunter said, "Who are you?"

Spirit Hunter says nothing.

In a blink of an eye, Light Hunter immediately swung his sword cutting deep into a body part of Dark Hunter's skin. Dark

Hunter screamed in pain and started swinging his sword inflicting severe wounds to the body of Light Hunter. But, luckily for Light Hunter because with him moving back a little, it only grazed his leg, but the sword was quite heavy that it did leave a deep cut within the wound. Light Hunter rapidly falls down in agony holding his leg as Dark Hunter puts a sword up to Light Hunter's face.

Light Hunter turned right to see his sword, but Dark Hunter's blade kept getting closer and closer to his face.

"It's time you die!" shouts Dark Hunter.

Light Hunter feels that all hope is lost, then a blade sliced the skin on the back on Dark Hunter's neck.

Dark Hunter screamed in pain, "AGHHHHH!!!!!"

Then Light Hunter grabs his sword and hit the dark sword, slowing it down from impact. Dark Hunter moves slightly to the left while getting back up, and then all three, Light Hunter, and Spirit Hunter vs Dark Hunter battling hard and strong, and moving around in the room chaotically, swords clinging and clashing, trying to get at Spirit Hunter. Spirit Hunter turns, raising his sword in an angled position making powerful blows, but Dark Hunter blocks his attack. Light Hunter's sword making contact breaking Dark Hunter's sword. Dark Hunter looking at his broken sword in disgust turns himself into shadow spirits, and scatters away in flight. Light Hunter looked at his sword and then he looks at the Spirit Hunter. Spirit Hunter's skin is light-red and his eyes are gray, but the red turns into white skin, like Light Hunter who is standing before him, but with grey eyes.

"Spirit Hunter what is your name?"

Spirit Hunter said nothing, remaining silent for the moment.

"Well, can you talk?" Light Hunter begins to move a little closer, but Spirit Hunter raises his sword. Light Hunter stopped and realizes that he's scared. So Light Hunter just stands there.

The Light Hunter said, "Thanks for helping." Spirit Hunter did nothing, so Light Hunter again spoke up, "You're just born scared and confused, I will show you how to overcome it right away."

Finally, Spirit Hunter speaks, asking, "You mean right away?"

Light Hunter with a sigh of relief replies, "Here, I will train you how to become a good Hunter." Light Hunter presented a soft smile with his arm extending without his sword in a gesture. "You will be my apprentice."

Reaching out with his hand, Spirit Hunter asks, "What is my name?"

The Light Hunter thinks for a minute, snaps his fingers as the ideal came up and said, "Your name is Evil Hunter."

"Hum . . . I like that name."

Evil Hunter and Light Hunter then

turned into spirits and went inside Hunter who is laying on the table about to undergo surgery.

The engineers went inside Hunter's upper part of his arm while the other engineer is holding the new arm for Hunter while the other engineer on the right side grabs the saw and makes a small incision on the inside of the arm putting a chip in it, and then connecting the sockets of his flesh-bone with the cyborg arm.

CHAPTER 5

Hunter, Vision and Nightmare

Hunter opens his eyes and felt the cold aluminum plated surgery table pressing up on his back. As he begins to start moving a bit he realizes that he's feeling nothing on his right arm, Hunter looked round and only saw the two engineers. One of the engineers turned around said, "Good morning sir, how are you feeling?

With a reply, Hunter said, "I'm fine."

Getting up, he feels metal movement, then looked at his cyborg arm. The second Engineer said your new arm has new weapons in it. Hunter looked at his arm then asked about what type of weapons were inside of his new cyborg arm.

The First Engineer said, "Well, the knife is under your wrist, but when you make a fist and wait for a little bit it'll spring right out almost spontaneous. Hunter then raises his fist for about a minute then the knife comes out. Hunter was amazed by what he saw.

Then, the Second Engineer said, "We

added flame with it as well."

Hunter then shoots out the flame for a little bit, then stops. Hunter repositioned himself so he can get off the table, moving his legs out so he can stand up.

Hunter asked, "Can I leave?" Both engineers looked at each other, then simultaneously said, "Yes, you can leave."

Hunter, looks back down at his cyborg arm, then back up at the engineers, smiled and began walking out of the building from the engineer's workplace.

Hunter soon walks around the hallway, staring at the hallway's hospital type looking colors; white, blue, and with the floor being gray. For a brief second, Hunter closes his eyes to get his bearings together, but just then he hears a girl crying. Hunter at once reopens his eyes, not believing what he's seeing his lover slowly dying. A part of her body had been ripped off and replaced with a cyborg body. Then, next thing he sees is a skull on the ground and then a voice coming out of nowhere. Hunter asking himself why this is happening, then tries to snap himself out of it. A couple of minutes had passed, and he now realizes what this nightmare vision meant. Hunter looking at his new cyborg arm - now transforming into human skin continued walking out of the building through the front doors and into the streets where he sees some mother and her children and a couple of guards walking to her nest. Hunter realizes it's getting very late, nighttime is settling in and noticing that he's walking down a back street.

CHAPTER 6
Back On War

Hunter was walking down the back road not seeing anything at first. He kept some of the Queen's Soldiers that were walking out of the nests. Still hearing the cries of pups, Hunter feels something is wrong, but Hunter kept walking. Hunter finally made it to his training facility. When he started opening the door it was very dark to see, but the lights automatically turned on as he continued walking in. Hunter was very tired and seeing his riverbed, he went directly to it and fell fast asleep.

The next day as Hunter woke up, he was feeling a little hungry and went to the mess hall to eat. After finishing his meal, he soon realizes that something is still wrong and that the queen is here. When Hunter was done, he went to the queen's castle.

Hunter greeted by the guard who was to let him in, and from a distance the queen noticed it was Hunter and was happy to see him. The queen sitting on the throne in a very large high-back chair notices Hunter's new cyborg arm and the Queen asked, "How's it working out for you, Hunter?"

Hunter looks up at the queen and said, "It is good my Queen."

The queen smiled and says, "Hunter, now you are my warrior whom can to fight everything in this battle, and I want you to take over under the Queen rule."

"Yes, my Queen," Hunter responded.

"Good, I need you to go back to earth."

"My Queen, yes!" Hunter replied.

Gracefully and with authority, the queen smiles and looks directly into his eyes. "Now take your ship and your men, and all the rest of the forces and I want you to kill every human on that planet called Earth."

Hunter on one knee looks up. "Yes, I will, as it is ordered. But Queen, if there is a god or goddess can you kill them?"

"Hunter," with this cold smile across her face, "I want you to destroy everything in its path and rule over anything that you get! You will rule all the worlds under my ruling!"

Hunter then stood back up at attention looking straight forward. "Yes, my Queen!"

The queen looked at him, again with this smile of a hardened hatred for Earth and said, "Oh yes, you will."

Hunter again responding, "Yes, my queen, as you command."

The queen's face turned back to normal then she said, "I also want you to go to Traverse City and destroy the last of the rebellion."

"Yes, my Queen. Consider it done!" Hunter then walks away from the queen as she signals him to carry out her orders, and then Hunter went directly to his ship; that was just at the middle of the queen's landing pad.

Hunter walking inside his ship.

"Hello Hunter, where are we going?"

"We're going to Traverse City," Hunter stated as he straps to a seatbelt to himself into the ship's Commanders seat in and the controls for launch. "Let's put an end to the rebellions. I command you to call the soldiers," replied Hunter.

The ship's voice had a slight pause then said, "Well I can't."

"Ship, why not?" with a little discuss from Hunter.

The ship in return said, "Some soldiers disappeared, some died in battle, and some of the others are gone."

Hunter said, "What about their families, can you get them?"

Ship said, "I can't."

CHAPTER 7
Battle of Traverse City

As the ship broke through the clouds, bullets were flying everywhere. Hunter was at the front of the ship's door. The doors to the ship lowering down as they're about to touch down with only a few 1,000 feet from the ground. When the door became fully opened, Hunter saw on the battleground humans combatting against the Queen's

Soldiers, some died of gunshot wounds, and others by the sharp blade of knives. The soldiers suffered deep flesh wound piercings of claw scratches. In the mist of battle through the flying bullets, Hunter wasted no time, he dropped out of the ship - air falling, hitting the ground hard as he was surrounded by a bubble shield for protection, only leaving a small crater.

The humans and the Queen's Soldiers immediately stopped at a quick pause, gazes over towards the one who made the crater. Just then, it was that opportune time, Hunter raised his left arm and bent his wrist downward clinching his fingers making a fist. The soldiers were still in a trance, marveling the way Hunter came down, Hunter's machine blaster came out and started shooting rock solid ice balls. The solid ice balls were hitting the human bodies in the field, leaving a little relief and resistance for the Queen's Soldiers. The humans were in anger and terror of being hit by these dangerous ice balls. They turned their guns towards Hunter and started shooting, but Hunter's bubble shield popped up in protection, reflecting the bullets which are now penetrating the human flesh. It was ripping and shredding the human body. Other humans were looking in amazement seeing and hearing their own bullets flying pass them. The other human bodies got torn apart.

More and more humans were firing

back in retaliation but they were dying every few minutes; bodies plopping to the ground all over the battlefield. Hunter unbending his fist and opening up his hand as the machine blaster retracts back into his arm while the knife begins to extend.

Five humans had ran toward Hunter, then one by one, neck, chest, arm, and legs started to rip off, some with even their throats cut. It was lightning fast. After the last wielding thrust from Hunter's knife, other humans ran out to grab the wounded. The queen's troops still wanting to fight even with missing limbs, but they were no match for Hunter. So, they carried them off the battlefield while the other humans continued to pull back.

Hunter and the Queen's Soldiers ran towards them when all the humans that were remaining in the fight were also finally pulling back as well.

Later on, Hunter was inside the ship looking at the map and planning the next attack.

Hunter asked the ship, "Do you see any humans attacking us yet?"

"No Hunter," replied Ship.

Then Hunter had felt like something or someone he loved was slowing dying, . . . "Oliva."

Hunter wondered if something was going on.

Ship said, "Hunter, start the attack!"

Then, Hunter snapped out of it. "Okay,

I'm coming!"

"Are you okay?" questioned Ship.

"Yes-yes, I'm fine." Hunter walked away then closed the hologram down.

As he was walking, out of nowhere a large blasting sound rippling through the air, hearing the gunshot roar behind Hunter. Hunter quickly turned around and saw two human girls; one got shot in the chest, and the other looked like she was holding a gun. The second girl was pointing it directly at Hunter through the opening of the ship's door. Hunter looked at the one human girl and began running towards her to kill her, but then a voice came out of nowhere, "Use your scream."

Hunter now being so confused

opened his mouth and started screaming. The scream became a force of strong wind that came out of his mouth pushing back the two girls, killing off the one who was already shot, and the other just got knockout.

Then the Queen's Soldiers ran inside the ship with their swords up, and they saw Hunter, and the soldiers were in shock – looking at what just happened. The Queen Commander walked in right behind them.

"Good job Hunter, we can take her to Slave Island."

Yes, my Queen," Hunter responded in gratitude and with a serious tone. "Yes, take her to Slave Island like the others."

The Commander then tells the soldiers to take her away. As the soldiers grab the female prisoner taking her away, Hunter begins to feel that something is still wrong, like he needed to go to Crystal Palace. But, Hunter felt something even far more stronger, then the voices; screams of the citizens, mothers and their pupps - screaming and crying.

Hunter tells the ship, "Go back to the Queen Republic, NOW!!!"

CHAPTER 8

Tragedy of Mothers

The ship landed on the clouds and then opened its big doors. Hunter got out and sneaks by two guards as they kept watch, but Hunter takes ahold of where the pupps hid, and ran out where they can see their father. Hunter then went out to see the city which was on a great depression state.

Unfortunately, only eight people were

there. Hunter continued walking through the city where he saw pupps crying, and then he saw where other mothers and pupps were hiding.

Hunter yelled out to the mothers and their pupps, "Hey, what happened?" But no one said anything. Hunter then ran through the city where the queen's front doors open. The guards were present throughout the castle. The door opened right away.

Hunter ran in and asked, "My Queen, are we under attack?"

The queen sitting in her chair looked down, then Hunter looked round and noticed that there were twenty chairs. Hunter then looked at the queen.

The queen then looked up at Hunter

and said, "Warriors, today we will make allies with the people who want to take over the Earth. Today our republic will be a reign of terror, tomorrow we are going to have a party of allies."

Hunter blurted out, "My Queen, what about the families?"

The queen did not say anything at first, then she said, "Go back to your training area and wait for the next mission."

Hunter looking at the queen knew she was not going to answer. So, Hunter said, "Yes, my Queen," then started walking towards the doors and the guards opened them letting Hunter walk out.

While walking all the way to his training place, Hunter then began thinking about "Maybe I should ask Jeilrenth what's going on." Hunter began running and continued running all the way to the barracks. When Hunter made it past the empty nests, he was right in front of the training entrance but stopped mid-way because he saw the motionless body of Jeilrenth laying there. Hunter quickly ran up to him and drop down, then held Jeilrenth and began to cry. Jeilrenth with his last strength looked up to see Hunter. He smiled then said, "Hunter, tomorrow you must leave and save these pups because . . ." Jeilrenth, now lay there dead exhaling his last dying breath. Hunter got up and forced open the door and hurried inside. It was a mess. Hunter again asking himself about what happened. Just then, he heard someone is coming so Hunter hid. The Queen's Soldiers came walking in and with the Commander Aziz in front.

Commander Aziz said, "Okay, make sure if there are rebels here, kill them."

Hunter realizing what he said jumped out from where he was hiding and yelled, "What kind of fishing are you doing?!"

The Queen's Soldiers pulled out their swords, but Commander Aziz said, "Hunter, the queen ordered us to search your barracks."

Hunter asked, "Then why is my mentor dead?"

Commander Aziz said, "The Queen and her advisors found out that he works with rebels. He tried to bomb the queen's castle."

Hunter asked what happened to the mothers and their pups, and Commander Aziz and the Queen's Soldiers froze on what Hunter said. Suddenly, Commander Aziz told the Queen's Soldiers to kill Hunter. When seven of the Queen's Soldiers pull out their swords then Hunter bent his wrists up extracting the knife; getting it to come out. Then Hunter jumped on one of the Queen's Soldiers cutting his neck killing him fast, then stabbing another in between the eyes before pulling back to avoid getting hit by the blades of the remaining Queen's Soldiers. However, a few swords wielding wildly in the air still came down on Hunter, but the bubble shield popped up and deflected the blows causing injuries to the soldiers, slicing their own skin.

Hunter knew that reinforcements were coming, so he thought of a plan but not so long before he could see what he could do to end this faster. Then he executed his move. Hunter ran as fast as he could into the last remaining Queen's Soldiers with his knife still protruding out from his wrist with his arms extended from an all-out battle. Hunter jumped up and did a backspin kicking his left leg into the head of one queen's soldier rendering him helpless, then grabbed his arm and pulling it out of his socket. Hunter thrusted upward into the jugular with his knife, lifting the queen's soldier off his feet, rendering an instant death. Then

Hunter flips over another Queen's Soldiers while retracting his knife and clinching his fist to extend out the blaster star-torch from his arm, now blazing the last remaining Queen's Soldiers that are combatting against him, Hunter killed the last queen's soldier and Commander Aziz.

Hunter stop blasting the fire, seeing that everything was charcoaled and noticed the sound of a nearby ship approaching, almost over the top of him. So, Hunter ran as fast as he could to get out of harm's way.

The ship opened a small square door on the bottom hull and released a tracking missile aimed at this building where Hunter was running past, then . . .

"BOOM!!!"

A huge bomb exploded. The fire growing to a blaze where whomever was in the vicinity could see it reaching to the sky. Hunter was making a safe escape. Hunter was now exhausted and looking to find a place to rest.

CHAPTER 9

Rise of The Rebellion

Hunter wakes up and to see the leaves falling. Then, realizes that he overslept because it was at the twilight of the day. Hunter finally gets up and started scouting throughout the city, walking everywhere. As he was going through the city, he notices the emptiness at several back areas on several outskirts of the city.

Hunter continued walking until he came to an abandon building. Over to the side of the building he saw a human truck, and pupps loading stuff into it. Then Hunter felt something in his pocket, so he went into his pocket and pulled out a hologram. Hunter played it, and what he saw was something that horrified him, then he looked back at the pupps still loading. While he was in deep thought, there was something obscure; vaguely off to the side of his peripheral vision. Hunter turned his face toward whatever it is that has now got his attention.

Looking in that direction there was a chikfactst walking up the middle of the road to the human truck. All pupps stopped and looked at Hunter, same with chikfactst pupp.

Then, she gave him this cold stare.

Hunter looked directly into her eyes and said, "I'm not going kill you or your pups."

The pupps' chikfactst replied, "Then why are you here?"

Hunter responded, "I think I was sent here by Jeilrenth for the rebellion."

Chikfactst had this worried look on her face, then said, "Hunter is Jeilrenth alive?"

Hunter looking down sadly and said, "No, he's dead."

Every pupp that heard this dropped everything that they were doing, and just then Chikfactst said, "Do they know that we're here?"

Hunter looked around at all of them then stated, "So, you are the rebels that he talked about."

Chikfactst ask again, "Did they know that we are here?"

"No, their dead - all of them," replied Hunter.

Every pupp looked at Hunter with confusion, then one of the pupps named Tmacho walked up next to Chikfactst, and when Hunter saw him he recognized who he was, then asked, "Are you that soldier who saved my life?"

Tmacho look at Hunter then replied, "Yes, I am the one who saved you from that explosion."

"What's your name?"

Someone came out from the crowd of pupps and yelled out, "Tmacho! . . . His name is Tmacho!" Then a pupp came up to the front and said, "My name is Mikey."

Hunter turned towards the right to look at Chikfactst, then asked, "What is your name Chikfactst?"

"Beretta."

Then out of nowhere a voice came shouting out among the crowd, "We can't trust him!!!" while he was still walking out from the shadows.

Mikey then turned to look at the one pupp who is still approaching then questioned, "What is the meaning of this; what do you mean we can't trust him?"

The pupp said, "He killed a lot of

humans and he's working with the Queen Republic."

Hunter said with a serious tone, "Look who's talking? I found this in his pocket." Then reached into his own pocket and pulled out this hologram projection disc and pressed play.

[Queen]: "You, Zacloge will become an undercover spy of the new rebellion. When they call us then, I'll send my rebel's killer to kill them. You got That?!"

[Zacloge]: "Yes, my queen!"

Hunter's hologram began repeating itself until he pressed the button again in order to make it stop. Zacloge knew he just got caught.

Then out of nowhere Zacloge pulled out a gun, pointed it at Hunter and began shooting, but every bullet that hit Hunter disappeared, then Zacloge felt the bullets inside of him. He then fell down to his death.

All the pupps were looking at this dead corpse lying on the ground. They then turned their attention toward Hunter, staring in amazement at his dark blue bubble shield. Hunter turned around and yelled, "Ok pupps, let's load up that truck right now!"

The pupps were hurrying as fast as they could to get their armour and personal protection in the truck. Hunter looked at Mikey and Beretta, then he asked, "Who's the leader of the rebels?"

Beretta exclaimed, "That would be me!"

Hunter looked at Beretta. "Why?"

"Well Hunter, I don't know you, but this queen is stealing our fathers and have an unspeakable breed or force breed. Then the queen orders our fathers and the Queen's Soldiers to kill the mothers and their pups. I was with my mother when I saw them come in. My mother tried to hold them off, but I escaped. The last thing I heard from my mother was her telling me to be strong, and to do the right thing."

Hunter seeing Beretta's face looked like she was going to cry, but then, Mikey held her arm as she looked into his eyes; he then glared back into hers.

While everyone was occupied getting things together and still loading up the truck, a ship's sound came out of nowhere. Hunter looked up and saw a ship directly on top of them, hovering over their heads.

"Ship! What are you doing here?! You're going to get us caught!" yelled Hunter.

The ship's two big doors opened, and a dragon flew out. Hunter couldn't believe what he was seeing.

Hunter said to himself "Night." Night flew towards Hunter and crashed into him, causing Hunter to be on the bottom and Night pressing down on top. Night started licking his face as the other pupps just looked and said nothing, well at least not out loud, under their breath they thought this is a black dragon, or he has a pet.

Hunter, with this big ole grin on his face said to Night, "Okay-okay! . . . Night, okay that's enough!"

Night got off Hunter, letting him get up.

Beretta and Mikey look at Hunter while he began standing and brushing himself off. Hunter looked over at them, shrugged his shoulders and said, "It's a long story."

One of the pupps walked over to Mikey and Beretta. They talked for a while. Hunter got done with his pet, Night. Hunter turned around and notices them having a very long conversation. Beretta walk up to

Hunter and said, "Hunter, go see the queen and find out who's her spy - so we need to move fast."

Hunter responded, "Then, we don't need to take the truck."

Beretta was concerned. "What about our stuff in that truck?"

Hunter look up and yelled, "Hey ship, land. You need to help these pupps pack it all in!"

Beretta looking back at Hunter. "What if this ship has a trap?"

Hunter said, "She can't betray us."

"Why?" responded Beretta.

"Because, it's my ship."

The ship landed and Hunter yelled at the pupps around the area, "Okay, go ahead and get your stuff out of the truck and put them inside ship. If the queen finds out our plans, it's not going to take long before the troops arrive. We need to move now!" Every pupp grabbed their stuff and walked inside the ship.

Beretta ask Hunter, "What is you plan?"

Hunter said, "Confronting the queen . . . and tonight, it's a party!"

Later at the queen's castle, the queen is sitting on her throne having a drink, strawberry dragon fruit wine, and there were other bad guys enjoying themselves as well.

But then, "BOOM!!!"

An explosion made a big hole through

one of the walls of the palace. The ship's two doors open, and Hunter is in the middle with Mikey on the right of the ship, and Beretta on the left. The queen got up and looked at Hunter, and then she saw his dragon behind him making raging noises.

"Calm down," said Hunter.

"What's this about?!" The queen angrily replied.

Hunter with a serious tone said, "You are under arrest for murdering families."

The queen looked at the two guards and made a head sign to tell them to deal with him. Two queen guards pulled out their sword and walked toward the ship. Hunter's knife came out and then he flew into the air and stabbed one of the guards on top of his head, and pulled it back out, killing him fast. Then Hunter went to the next guard, jumped up and sliced his head off.

The queen knows she's going to die by him, so the queen clasped her hands together forging a ray of lightning that was coming out of her hands, aiming it directly at Hunter.

When Hunter sees it, he raises his hand causing the knife to go back in, and then spreading his own fingers where he produces lightning to come out as well; beginning a duel of lightning strikes against the queen.

In the heat of the battle, the bolts of lightning began hitting each other hard, each one pushing out some heavy power. Hunter was shocked that he was able to make lightning come out of his fingers.

Then, Hunter somehow heard the Queen's Soldiers coming, so Hunter closed his eyes and then lightning grew more powerful causing the queen to lose her strength in the fight.

"THRASSSHHH – BOOOOMMM!!!"

Hands glowing so bright until the decaying of this extraordinary display of lights began to diminish with each blow. The rays were striking into each other, back and forth until there was nothing left. Their lightning showdown had almost stopped immediately as the queen was pushed really hard from the impact, knocking her back. Hunter began running toward the ship and finally was able to get on it before the queen picked herself up off the ground. The queen hears the roaring sound of the ship's engines, looks up as it passes by upon its takeoff.

Hunter and the other pupps that were standing in one area of the ship while the others are sitting down were thinking about, "What's next?" Just then, one of the ship's computers started beeping. Hunter ran toward it to see why it was sounding.

Then Hunter looked to see and said, "Incoming beam heading toward earth."

The ship opened its backdoors. Hunter and the pupps saw the purple and red color mixed beams heading toward earth. It hit like a volcano; exploding a heatwave of wire across the planet. The next thing that happened on earth was a strong heavy gush of fire spreading all around that soon turned into hot molding lava.

Hunter said, "Ship, do we have a way out before we get caught by the Queen Republic?"

The ship closed the backdoor and then said, "Hold on." The ship started flying forward, and then into an unknown portal.

CHAPTER 10

New Home

When the ship came out from within the portal, Hunter looked at one of the computers to see if he can still see the planet Earth.

Hunter asked, "Where are we ship?"

The ship said, "We're in an unknown universe."

The pupps began looking at the main

controls of where the head is.

Hunter said, "Don't worry, it's safe."

The ship continued its analysis, "What if I found out that earth is not ruled by humans or animals, just a forest of non-living creatures."

Hunter looked at the ship's computer head and said, "This is good."

Beretta asked, "Why is this good?"

Hunter replied, "We need to be hidden so no one will ever know where we are, and our blood creates life. So, when we land, we are going to build a new home . . ."

The ship was cordially interrupted with making another assessment of the situation. "I have to drop you and the pupps off to make sure that we're not actually being followed."

Hunter was shocked at what he heard. Looking around the room of the ship, he sees that other pupps were in shock, also.

"Ship, what if we need air support or . . ."

"No need. You'll be fine. Plus, I think you are the protector of this new group of rebels," replied Ship.

Hunter looked around and had noticed that Mikey, Beretta, and other pupps were looking at him with confidence.

Hunter then tells the ship to make a landing and to leave them there; to make sure no one from the Queen's Republic drop ship has come in to orbit or within the atmosphere. The ship agreed.

So, Hunter flew the ship towards Earth. When the ship made it pass the atmosphere, all the way down to the stratosphere, the ship landed itself on the ground. Hunter and other pupps walked out. When the last ones cleared out from the ship, the ship closed its doors and took off. Hunter looked at the pupps with all their protection and personal belongings that they had. Then Hunter said out loud, "Guys, get ready to go."

All pupps said, "Jod."

Everyone starts walking to where the flatlands were located and started a new home. It took them five days of walking, and then one night they stopped.

Hunter and pupps halted for a

moment and then Hunter yells to everyone, "Okay, we stop here for tonight!"

The pupps dropped their stuff and rested a bit. Hunter was hearing water falling from somewhere.

Another pupp named Drake spoke up and said, "Hunter, I think the humans call it a waterfall, but that's just what I heard."

Hunter agreed, and said, "Okay, who wants to shower tonight?"

So every pupp was ready to dive in except the last one, Beretta. Beretta rather go alone when she gets a chance to wash her own self privately, which is understandable. She also began drifting into memory, having thought of a time about her mother. When she came out of it, she looked up and saw someone over top of her, it was Mikey.

Mikey said, "Hey sweety."

Beretta yelled, "Mikey!"

Mikey look at her with this smile, and Beretta knew what he was thinking.

Beretta said, "I know I'm the last one in my family, and I know I want to be a mother."

"Are you sure you want to do emergency breeding?" asked Mikey.

Beretta blushed, then she said, "Yes!"

Back at the camp, Hunter and some of the other pupps were around the campfire talking, while others were doing their own thing.

Hunter said, "It's been hours. Where are they?"

Just then, you could see Mikey and Beretta walking out of the forest holding hands together and then sitting down by the campfire as well.

Hunter said, "Well anyway, I have not seen a ship in a couple of days."

One pupp said, "Maybe ship abandoned us."

Another one said, "No, maybe there are over one hundred Queen's Republics popping up in the middle of nowhere and then her ship did make the jump and started attacking."

Hunter responded, taking everything in notion, "Wherever the ship is, I just hope the ship is safe."

Every pupp looked at Hunter like if it

was the first time that he ever cared about something.

Then Hunter said, "Okay, let's get some rest."

So everyone fell asleep, then the next day Hunter and a small group of rebels walked the perimeters; it seemed like almost forever, but then, when it looked as though they were having to get back to the campfire, Hunter saw a flat Island where he knew they could make a new home.

Hunter was in the front, he turned around yelled, "This is it, our new home!"

Some pupps jumped and danced with so much joy, while others were very confused because they were satisfied with having the flatland without trees.

Hunter said, "This is where we build a new village or town."

Mikey responded, "Well, let's get started on it then."

Blaze said, "We did not bring any tools."

"Well then, I guess we'll have to make our own set of tools."

All the pupps were looking at Hunter.

Hunter said, "This planet will give us the resources that we can use." Hunter then turned around to the others and said, "Tell them to find something to make a building with, for now."

So, the pupps spread out to try and find materials to make tools. One pupp, Egan, found gray liquid and another named

Malinda found hard skinny brick size tools. Hunter and the other pupps tested out everything by setting it all up. It was a good thing, because it was night and it began raining and storming. Then the next day it stood the test, so they continued building.

Day 10, Hunter took a look at the wall, then he heard Mikey's voice. Hunter turned around to see what was going on. Beretta looked like she has a swollen belly as she was sleeping.

Mikey said to Hunter, "She . . ."

Hunter Interrupted him by saying, "You're going to have a pupp."

Mikey knew that Hunter knows she is pregnant because everyone knew the scent that her body was giving off.

A few minutes later, the ship showed up behind Hunter and the pupps. The ship then landed.

Hunter said to himself to whoever could hear him, "Life will fall but there will always be light. Light itself is nothing at first, but when it Sparks new hope will rise. We don't know when it is going to Spark again. But, after the rise of the New Republic, to take down Queen Republic, we are that New Hope."

Mikey asked Hunter, "So, what do we call our new republic?"

Hunter said, "Hunter Republic! And I want you and Beretta to be second to rule with me."

Mikey then stated, "I thought when

you killed Zacloge, we'd lose our power."

Hunter laughed and said, "No, I made both of you power. You two are second in command to lead the new republic because we can't beat the Queen Republic now. We need allies to take down the Queen Republic. So, when this town is up, I need to start looking for allies."

Mikey asked, "Are you leaving us?"

Hunter looked at him. "No, of course not. I'm just looking to find new allies that will help us grow."

"Well, this means that you will be our king," responded Mikey.

Hunter said, "No king or queen, or even president."

Mikey asked, "Then, what is it?"

Hunter said, "I don't know, I need to think about it."

Hunter and Mikey looked over the new city and its capital of the Hunter Republic as the sun was coming down to make dawn.

"Life will fall but there are always light. Light itself, it is nothing at first, but when it Sparks new hope will rise. We don't know when it is going to Spark, but after the rise of the new republic to take down the Queen Republic, we are the new hope to us and other universes, and dimensions. These are dark times, but where there is darkness, there will always be light."

CPSIA information can be obtained
at www.ICGtesting.com
Printed in the USA
BVHW030216200323
660778BV00004B/131

9 781946 746870